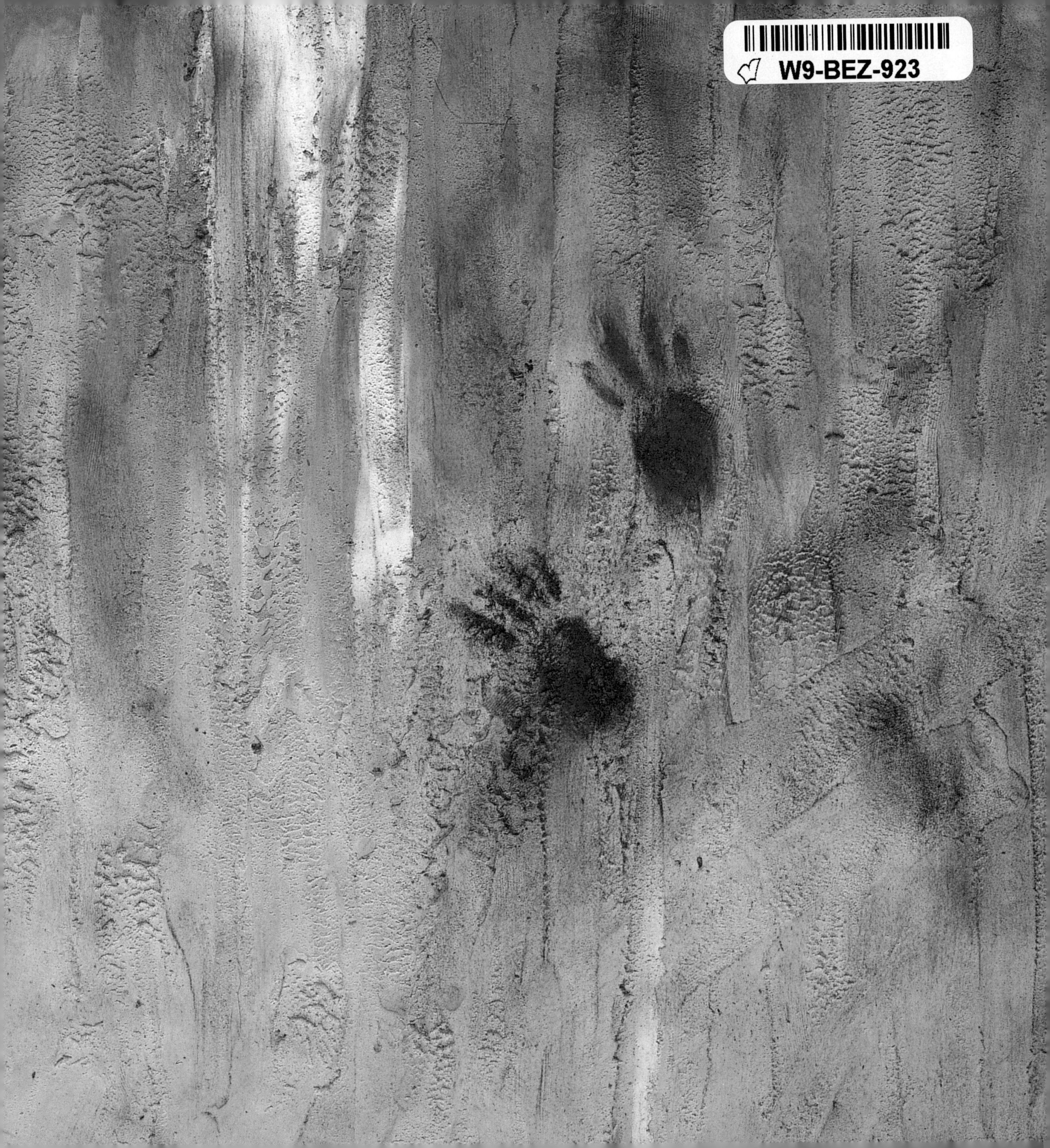

For Kyle
Christmas 2003
From Uncle Rob, Auntie Paula
& Cousin Simon

THE SUBWAY MOUSE

The illustrations for this book were made with Plasticine
that is shaped and pressed onto illustration board.
Acrylic paint, found objects and other materials are used for special effects.

The type in this book was set in 16 point Gararond Medium.

Photography by Ian Crysler.

National Library of Canada Cataloguing in Publication

Reid, Barbara, 1957-
Subway mouse / Barbara Reid.

For ages 4-9.
ISBN 0-439-97468-2

1. Mice--Juvenile fiction. I. Title.

PS8585 E4484 S82 2003 jC813'.54 C2003-901056-2
PZ7

6 5 4 3 2 Printed and bound in Canada 03 04 05 06 07

THE SUBWAY MOUSE

Barbara Reid

North Winds Press
A Division of Scholastic Canada Ltd.

For Mum, love always.
— B.R.

Nib was a subway mouse.

He was born into a large family that lived below the platforms in a busy subway station.

The mice called their home Sweetfall.

While the trains thundered overhead, the grown-up mice gathered food. When the trains rested, they came home to their nests.

In the quiet, the old mice told stories. Stories about Tunnel's End: a dangerous, roofless world filled with mouse-eating monsters. But Tunnel's End was also beautiful. The air was sweet. A brave mouse could find the tastiest foods, the softest nests.

Storytime was Nib's favourite time of day.

When he grew big enough to hunt for food, Nib explored the station floor. He found strange things, beautiful things and things that reminded him of his favourite stories.

He started to bring these things home.

"Your garbage is crowding our babies!" the mothers complained.

"Your babies are nibbling my stuff!" Nib answered.

Then he had an idea.

He found an empty corner and built a snug hideout. Nib loved to come home, wash up and fall asleep surrounded by his colourful treasures.

He travelled to Tunnel's End in his dreams.

One night, Nib came home to a mess.

"Nice place!" said his cousin Carmel.

"We fixed it up," added Ripper.

"Got anything to eat?" asked Pit.

They stayed all night. Pit snored.

The coming rumble of the morning train woke the cousins. They scratched, stretched and scampered off.

"See you later, Nib!" said Carmel. "We'll bring Stinky and Crumbs tonight!"

A train pounded into the station in a cloud of dust. The brakes screamed.

"Another noisy day," thought Nib. "Another noisy, dirty, dull, grey day."

With a warning hiss the train tore out of the station. *Whoosh!* A gust of wind snatched up the pieces of Nib's ruined nest.

One tiny feather swirled and flew away down the tunnel and out of sight. Nib had another idea.

"Goodbye!" He trotted past his cousins. "You can have my nest. I'm going to Tunnel's End!"

"You'll starve!" said Pit.

"You'll be gobbled up!" said Ripper.

Carmel sniffed. "Tunnel's End? That's just an old mouse tale!"

The next train drowned out their laughter.

Nib counted five trains before he looked back. He had never been this far from home.

The tunnel stretched on. Nib curled in a crack to sleep.

He woke up stiff and sore. Jogging along, he tried not to think about food.

Up ahead the tunnel brightened. Nib started to run. Tunnel's End!

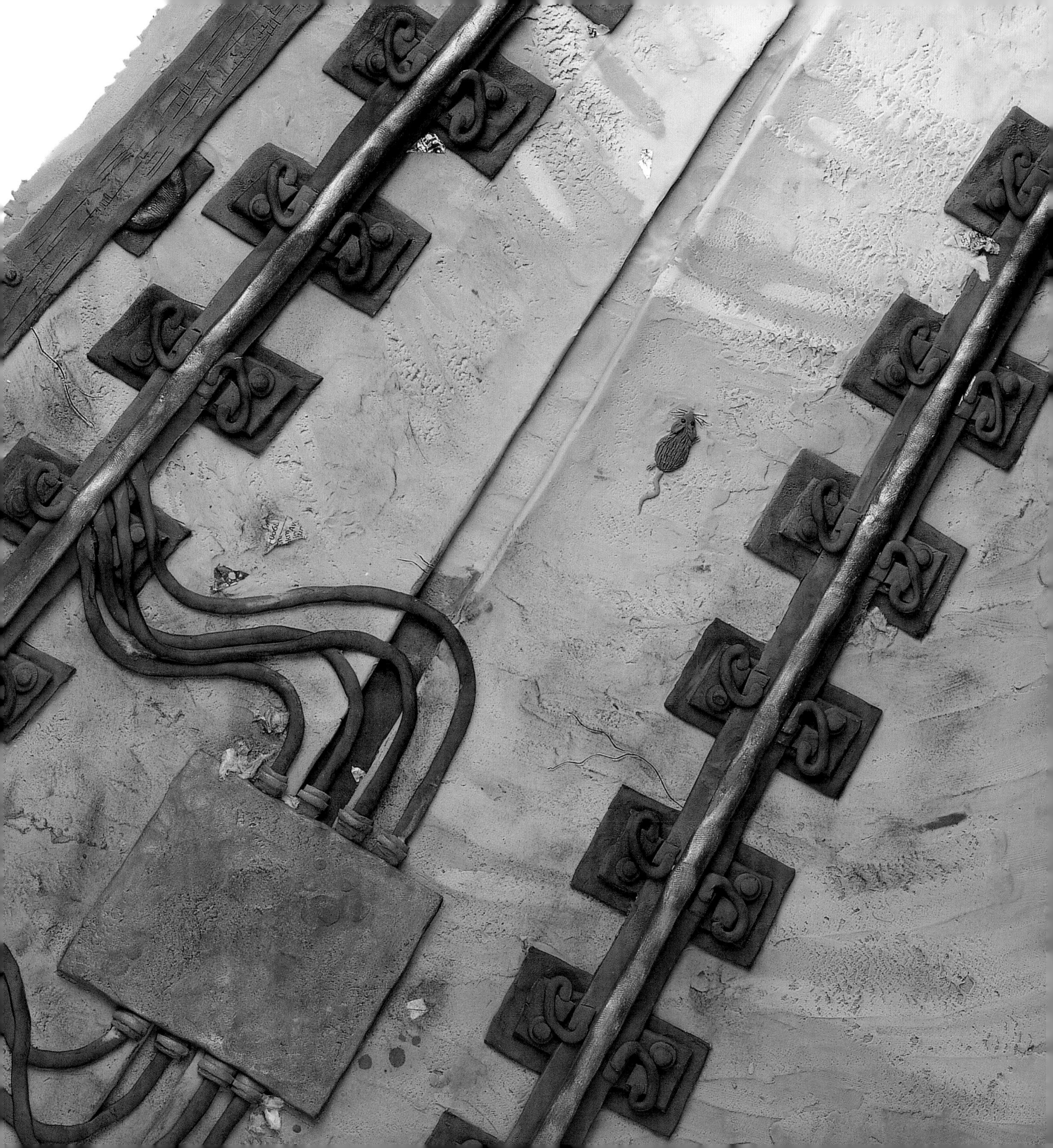

Reaching the light, Nib blinked. Was he back home?

"Who are you?"

Nib jumped. It was a strange mouse.

"My name is Nib." He pointed behind him. "I came from Sweetfall."

"Never heard if it!" said the strange mouse. "I'm Lola. This is Sugardrop."

Nib pointed ahead. "I'm going to Tunnel's End."

"Pooh!" said Lola. "That's just an old mouse tale."

"Well," said Nib, "at least you've heard of it."

A train came and went.

"Maybe I should come with you," Lola said.

"Maybe you should," said Nib, and started down the track.

"Hold it!" Lola caught a wrapper in mid-air. "No point travelling on an empty stomach."

They licked the paper clean. Together they passed out of Sugardrop into the next tunnel.

Many trains later, the mice reached another station. Nib saw a jellybean and pounced.

"Drop it!" A big mouse blocked their path. Two others stepped out from behind him.

"Run!" Lola squeaked.

Dodging and darting, they ran the length of the station, vith the gang snapping at their tails. They were far into he next tunnel before the cries of "Stop, thief!" died out.

Nib still had the jellybean.

But now there was no turning back.

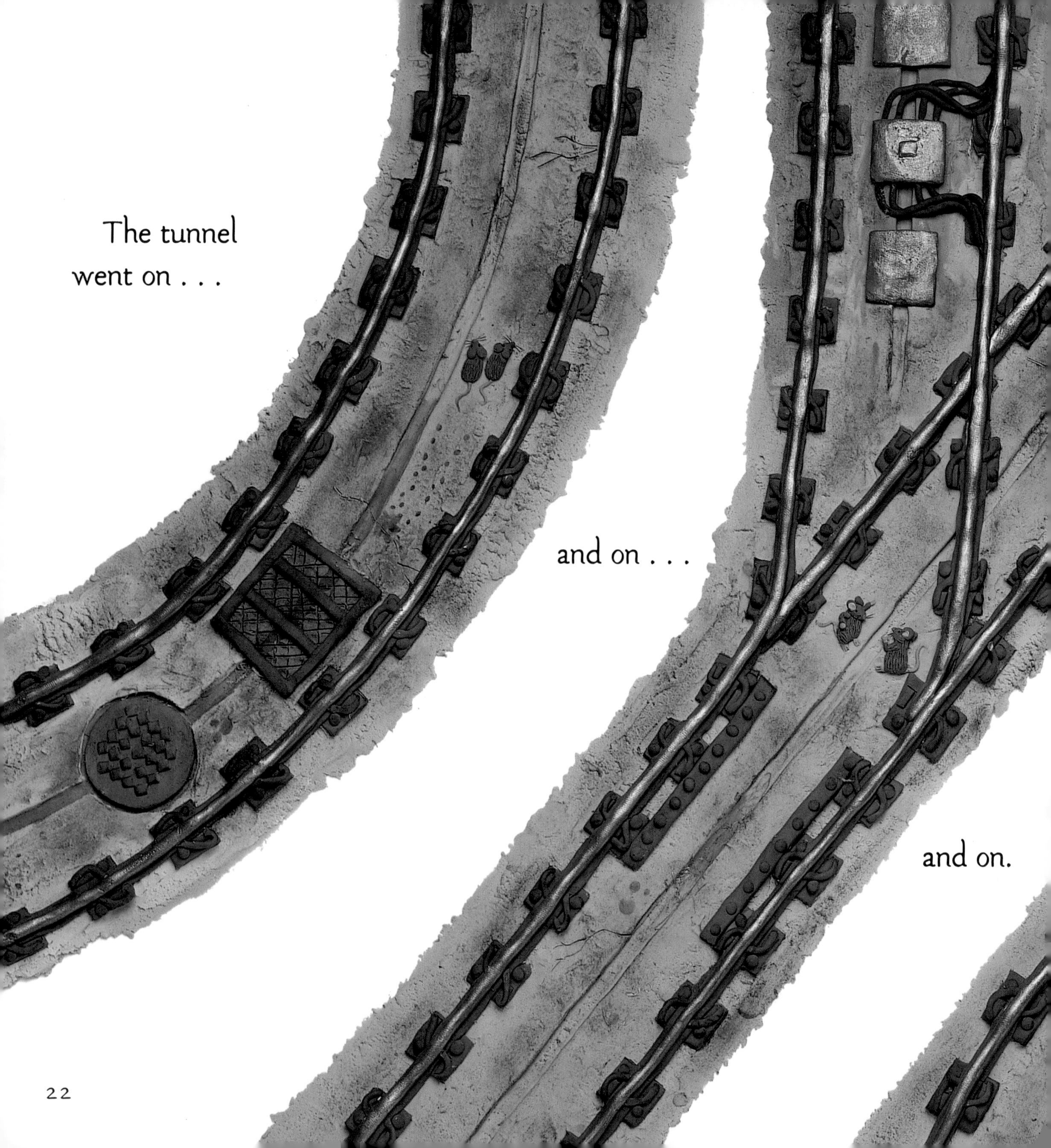

The tunnel
went on . . .

and on . . .

and on.

There were many stations. There was not much to eat.

As they plodded along another unending curve, the last train roared past.

There was no sign of a station.

Lola stopped.

“I’m worn thin! I’m hungry and thirsty and I need a rest in a nest. I quit!”
“There’s nothing here,” said Nib. “We have to go on.”
“I won’t,” said Lola. “Look, I’m making a nest!”

She plucked a feather from under the rail.
Nib knew it at once. "That's mine!" He grabbed for it.
"Finders keepers!" said Lola. She sat on it.

A tiny, far-off note echoed through the tunnel. Nib's fur stood on end. What was that?

Lola's eyes grew large.

Again they heard the small, musical chirp. They started toward the sound.

As they rounded the corner, a light breeze brushed their whiskers.

"Mmmmm," sighed Lola. "Sweet."

More voices joined the song. The tunnel widened to a soft light.

“Tunnel’s End,” breathed Nib.

N

“Come on!” Lola dove into the forest of wet grass. Nib chased after her. The mice raced to the hilltop, where they feasted on seeds, drank the dew and danced in the moonlight.

They slept right through the morning trains.

Tunnel's End was more dangerous than Nib had imagined.

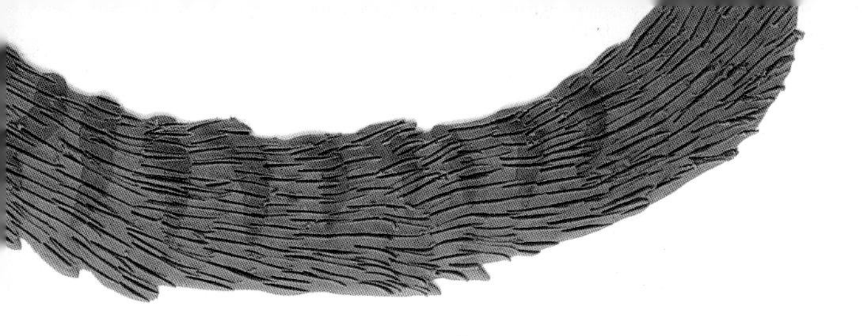

It was also more beautiful than he had dreamed.

Lola made herself at home. Later, as she tucked their mouse children into a snug nest, Nib told them stories.

It was their favourite time of day.

The End